## Read with Mummy

# Little Red Riding Hood

This paperback edition published in 2005 by
Armadillo Books
An imprint of Bookmart Ltd
Blaby Road, Wigston
Leicester, LE18 4SE

ISBN 1-84322-437-2

1 3 5 7 9 10 8 6 4 2

© 1999 Bookmart Limited

Originally published in hardback
by Bookmart Ltd in 1999

Printed in China

# Little Red Riding Hood

Story retold by Janet Brown
Illustrations by Ken Morton

ARMADILLO

A woodcutter and his wife live in a cottage at the edge of the forest. They have only one child, a happy little girl who is loved by everyone she meets.

The woodcutter's wife makes her daughter a special present – a beautiful red riding cape with a large hood.

Soon the girl is known to everybody as Little Red Riding Hood.

*Why does everyone call the woodcutter's daughter
Little Red Riding Hood?*

One day the woodcutter's wife bakes a cake and puts it in a basket with a bottle of lemonade.

"Your Grandmother has a bad cold," she tells Little Red Riding Hood.

"I want you to take her this cake and lemonade. Now go straight there and remember, don't stray from the path or talk to any strangers!"

*What is Little Red Riding Hood going to take to her poorly Grandmother?*

Little Red Riding Hood sets off happily along the path that runs deep into the forest. In the distance she can hear her father at work, chop-chopping with his axe. Suddenly a large, hungry wolf appears! He too hears the woodcutter in the distance, so he pretends to be friendly.

"Where are you going with that basket of food, my dear?" he asks.

Without thinking, Little Red Riding Hood replies, "I am taking it to my sick Grandmother."

"How kind!" says the sly wolf. "But if I were your Grandmother, I should like to have some pretty flowers as well, to cheer me up!"

*Why does the wolf pretend to be friendly to
Little Red Riding Hood?*

"What a good idea!" says Little Red Riding Hood.

So she strays from the path to pick some flowers for Grandmother.

She does not know that the wolf knows exactly where Grandmother lives!

She does not know that while she is lingering to pick flowers, the wolf is running silently through the forest to Grandmother's house!

What is the wolf doing whilst Little Red Riding Hood is picking flowers?

The wolf arrives long before Little Red Riding Hood. He knocks softly on the door. Grandmother is expecting a visit.

"Just lift the latch, dear!" she calls.

Then she sits up to put on her glasses – and catches sight of the wolf! She quickly jumps out of bed and hides in the cupboard.

Why does Grandmother hide in the cupboard?

The wolf sees the empty bed. He knows that Grandmother is hiding somewhere. But Grandmother is old and dry, and the wolf would much rather eat Little Red Riding Hood, who is young and juicy. So instead of searching the house, he puts on Grandmother's nightcap and glasses and climbs into the warm bed.

*Why do you think the wolf puts on Grandmother's nightcap and glasses?*

Little Red Riding Hood arrives with her gifts for Grandmother.

"Grandmother, what big, beady eyes you have!" she says in surprise.

"All the better to see you with, my dear!" replies the wolf.

"And what great, flapping ears you have!"

"All the better to hear you with, my dear!" replies the wolf.

"And what white, pointy teeth you have!"

"All the better to eat you with, my dear!" shouts the wolf and jumps out of bed!

*What three things does Little Red Riding Hood notice about "Grandmother"?*

"Help!" cries Little Red Riding Hood.

She screams so loudly that her voice carries over the trees. It carries deep into the forest where the woodcutter is sitting down to eat his lunch.

The woodcutter knows all the sounds of the forest. He knows the chirp of every bird, the squeak of every rabbit and the scream of every little girl that has ever been chased by a wolf! He drops his sandwich and leaps to his feet.

*What is the woodcutter doing when he hears Little Red Riding Hood's screams?*

The wolf is chasing Little Red Riding Hood around the bedroom. Suddenly the woodcutter comes running into the house swinging his axe! The wolf is so scared that he jumps out of the window and runs away.

The woodcutter hugs his daughter and they let Grandmother out of the cupboard. Then they sit down to eat the cake and drink the lemonade.

"I will never talk to strangers again," promises Little Red Riding Hood.

*What does Little Red Riding Hood promise never to do again?*

# On a piece of paper practise writing these words:

the sly wolf

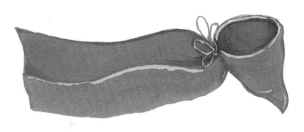

red cape and hood

forest

basket

night cap

Trace with your finger along the path and help Little Red Riding Hood find her way to Grandmother's house.